WELCOME  LD
OF
Geronimo Stilton

Published by Sweet Cherry Publishing Limited
Unit 36, Vulcan House,
Vulcan Road,
Leicester, LE5 3EF,
United Kingdom

First published in the UK in 2018
2018 edition

ISBN: 978-1-78226-372-2

Text by Geronimo Stilton
Art Director: Iacopo Bruno
Graphic Designer: Laura Dal Maso / theWorldofDOT
Original cover illustration by Roberto Ronchi and Christian Aliprandi
Concept of illustration by Roberta Bianchi, produced by Andrea Denegri and Valentina Grassini
with assistance from Lara Martinelli and Elisabetta Natella
Initial and final page illustrations by Roberto Ronchi and Ennio Bufi MAD5, Studio Parlapà and
Andrea Cavallini. Map illustrations by Andrea Da Rold and Andrea Cavallini.
Cover layout and typography by Elena Distefano
Interior layout and typography by Cecilia Bennett, Rhiannon Izard, and Amy Wong
Graphics by Marta Lorini
© 2013 Edizioni Piemme S.p.A., Palazzo Mondadori – Via Mondadori, 1 – 20090 Segrate
© 2017 English edition, Sweet Cherry Publishing
International Rights © Atlantyca S.p.A. – Via Leopardi 8, 20123 Milano, Italy
Translation © 2016, Atlantyca S.p.A.

Original title: *Lo strano caso dei brufoli blu*
Based on an original idea by Elisabetta Dami

With special thanks to the Umberto Veronesi Foundation

www.geronimostilton.com/uk

Printed and bound in Turkey

Geronimo Stilton

THE CHEESE EXPERIMENT

Sweet Cherry
Publishing

A SUPER-SPECIAL DAY

One cool and peaceful Monday in late September, I woke up early, stretched my paws over my head, and got ready for a SUPER–SPECIAL day ...

Oops, I'm sorry – I forgot to introduce myself! My name is Stilton, *Geronimo Stilton*. I'm the editor of The Rodent's Gazette, the most famous newspaper on Mouse Island.

I brushed my teeth with cheesemint toothpaste. Yum!

Brush, brush!

My job keeps me busy, but that morning I was headed to my nephew Benjamin's school for the opening of their new science labs. I was supposed to give a speech! I wanted to look **SOPHISTICATED** for four reasons:

1) To make my little nephew proud.

2) Because the school principal is a good friend of mine.

3) Because I knew that Dr. Margo Bitmouse — otherwise known as Doc — would be there. She's a marvemousely smart and *beautiful* rodent!

4) Because my grandfather had called and hollered,

I combed my fur with Sleekfur ...

I put on my freshly pressed suit ...

"Grandson! Did you comb your whiskers? Did you write a good speech? Don't be a **CHEESEBRAIN**. The reputation of The Rodent's Gazette is at stake!"

So I took a little longer than usual to make sure I looked **mouserific**. Finally, I checked myself in the mirror one last time and grinned. Not bad!

I hailed a taxi and headed to Benjamin's school. On the ride, I went over the speech in my head – but the closer we got to the school, the more my tail trembled and my whiskers wobbled! **Holey cheese, I was a wreck!**

The taxi driver was a rodent around Grandfather

I put on a red silk tie. Very fancy!

I sprayed myself with a hint of Parmesan cologne.

Aren't you Geronimo Stilton?

10.30

William's age. He was large and had a **THICK GREY HANDLEBAR MOUSTACHE**. He kept glancing at me in the rearview mirror.

At a red light, he turned to face me. "Aren't you Geronimo Stilton? The publisher of The Rodent's Gazette?"

I nodded. "Yes, that's me!"

"Mr. Stilton, your snout is as white as a slice of mozzarella cheese!" he said, looking worried. "Are you feeling okay? Are you getting **CARSICK**? There's a special sickness bag under the seat — I always keep a few handy for weak-stomached rodents like you."

I held up a paw and tried to reassure him. "Oh, it's

not car sickness. I promise. **I'm just nervous!** When I get to the school, I have to:

    1) walk a red carpet in front of hundreds of rodents (WITHOUT TRIPPING!),

    2) give a speech in front of hundreds of rodents and TV reporters (WITHOUT FORGETTING WHAT TO SAY!), and

    3) cut the inaugural ribbon for the new science labs (WITHOUT SNIPPING MY PAW!)"

The taxi driver raised an eyebrow and muttered, "Mr. Stilton, I assumed you were a brilliant, carefree mouse, like your grandfather William Shortpaws! I had the

pleasure of driving him around in my taxi quite often in the old days."

Cheese and crackers! I tried to justify myself.

"Well, usually ... I mean, sometimes ... actually ... I'm more or less an **EASY-GOING** mouse. But today I have to give a speech, and I'm so worried about it that my fur is standing on end! Excuse me ..."

I buried my snout in the pages of my speech.

"Humph, they don't make journalists the way they used to," the taxi driver grumbled. "Your grandfather William was a real journalist – not a **CHEDDARHEAD** like you!"

By now we had arrived at New Mouse City's primary school, the same school I went to as a mouseling. As I climbed out of the taxi, I noticed something weird. There were little blue clouds hovering in the air outside the school, and it STUNK of garlic!

Cheese niblets, how strange!

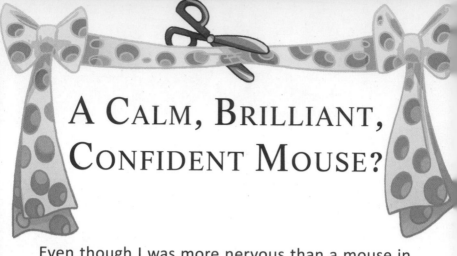

A CALM, BRILLIANT, CONFIDENT MOUSE?

Even though I was more nervous than a mouse in a room **FULL OF CATS**, the morning went well. I climbed the school steps without tripping and greeted my friend the principal with a polite kiss on the paw. *"You're such a gentlemouse, Geronimo!"* she squeaked.

I didn't freeze when I gave my speech, even though hundreds of reporters were watching and filming me for

Here I am!

Geronimo!

Smack!

all the TV stations on Mouse Island. I didn't get tongue-tied even once – a record for a **shy mouse** like me!

And when I cut the yellow ribbon to open the new ultra-modern science labs, I didn't nick my paws, snip off any whiskers, or get tangled up in the ribbon. **SLIMY SWISS CHEESE**, it was a miracle!

Was I finally becoming a calm, brilliant, and confident rodent?

I scurried into the new science labs, feeling marvemouse.

When the principal began showing us the new lab equipment, I stood up straight and held my snout **HIGH IN THE AIR**, just like a mouse who was calm, brilliant,

and confident ... but I didn't pay attention to the freshly waxed floor!

Proudly, I approached the principal to compliment her. "This lab is absolutely a state-of-the-art –"

I didn't have time to finish before I slipped on the waxed floor! After doing a **DOUBLE-TWISTED DEATH-DEFYING** SOMERSAULT, I ended up with my snout in the rubbish bin.

So much for being a calm, brilliant, confident mouse ...

I pulled my head out of the rubbish bin and saw

I'm so cool!

YIIIIKES!

SCIENCE LAB

SWISSHHH

the principal staring at me with a funny look on her snout. My face turned as **RED** as the tomato sauce on a **DOUBLE-CHEESE PIZZA**! I tried to crack a joke.

"I know it looks like I slipped, but, um, I was just making sure the floor was perfectly smooth!"

The principal raised an eyebrow. "What about diving into the **RUBBISH BIN**?"

Looking down at my paws, I muttered, "I was, uh, checking to see if it was empty ..."

She burst out laughing.

SQUEAK!

I felt like such a cheesebrain!

OHHHH...

OUCH! OUCH!

"Geronimo, you haven't changed a whisker since we were in primary school!"

And then – rat-munching rattlesnakes! – she kissed me lightly on the tip of my snout. Now I was red from the ends of my ears to the tip of my tail!

At that moment, I noticed something strange. **There was an enormouse blue spot on the principal's snout!**

Mouldy Mozzarella – A Blue Spot!

ROTTEN RATS' TEETH! An ugly blue spot had popped up on my friend's snout! It was so enormouse and so blue that I couldn't stop staring at it.

Tugging on her whiskers nervously, she asked, "Why are you staring at my snout?"

I didn't want to offend her, so I muttered, "Oh, I was just looking at your beautiful blue eyes ..."

"My eyes aren't blue," she said slowly. "They're black!"

WhOOPS.

She opened her purse, pulled out a mirror, and squeaked, **"THUNDERING CATTAILS** – what is that **BLUE SPOT**?"

A blue spot! Ack! Ack! Ack!

19

The principal looked like she was about to faint from shock.

A second later, I heard a loud squeak from another mouse.

"**MOULDY MOZZARELLA** – a BLUE SPOT!"

Then I heard another squeak … and another … and another!

"**RANCID RICOTTA** – a BLUE SPOT!"

For the love of cheese, what was happening?

Just then I felt an itch on my snout. Did I have a blue spot, too? While everyone headed off to grab refreshments, I scampered to the bathroom …

Phew, I was safe! No BLUE SPOTS! I headed back to the lab, but I couldn't help thinking that this whole thing was awfully strange.

And that's when I ran into my sister Thea – and Doc! Doc is a tough, energetic, intelligent, and

very beautiful rodent. She's **FABUMOUSE**! But every time I see her, I always get my tail in a twist and end up looking like a complete **CHEESEBRAIN**!

I was just hoping she hadn't seen my somersault – the one that ended with a **dive** into the rubbish bin. Maybe she had been looking the other way ...

Doc pinched my cheeks and squeaked, "Nice job, my little cheese puff – you gave a marvemouse speech And congrats on that tumble, too!" She winked.

SQUEAK!
I felt like such a CHEESEBRAIN!

Peering at my paws, I headed towards the refreshments with my **tail between my legs**. But when I got there, I forgot all about my embarrassment ... because most of the rodents near me were covered with BLUE SPOTS!

I scampered over to the principal and whispered, "Um, these BLUE SPOTS worry me!"

I lowered my voice even further. "Should we send everyone home? They could be contagious ..."

"You're right, Geronimo," she said, nodding her snout seriously.

She walked up to the microphone and announced, "Dear rodent friends, thank you for coming on this special day! Unfortunately, we have to bring the festivities to an end. It was wonderful seeing all of you. **Thank you, and goodbye!**"

An Enormouse Banana Ice Cream Cone

I took Benjamin's paw and headed out of the school. As we walked, he squeaked happily, "Uncle G, your speech was **awesome**!"

Next to him, Bugsy Wugsy chuckled.

"The best part, though, was the surprise ending when you dove into the rubbish bin!"

I pretended I hadn't heard her because Doc had just walked out of the school. She pinched me on the cheek again and said, "Nice job, my little cheese puff! The principal told me it was your idea to send everyone home. You're right – those **BLUE SPOTS** do seem contagious. Maybe you're not a **HOPELESS CHEDDARHEAD** after all ..."

Flustered, I blurted, "Oh, compliment for the thanks. I mean, thanks for the compliment, even if I'm not really, totally, completely sure that what you said was a compliment, because I have a feeling you just said I'm a **HOPELESS CHEDDARHEAD** ... but I always hope that I don't **look** like a Cheddarhead! Anyway, thanks!"

With that, Doc walked away, chuckling to herself.

I wanted to tear out my whiskers – but I couldn't let Benjamin and Bugsy see my frustration! So I tried

SQUEAK!

I felt like such a **CHEESEBRAIN!**

Um ...

Maybe you're not a hopeless Cheddarhead!

not to let my fur get ruffled. Instead, I said, "How about some ice cream?"

"Yes! **FABUMOUSE!**" Bugsy and Benjamin squeaked excitedly.

We went to the Icy Rat, which has the best ice cream in New Mouse City. We sat down at a small table and each ordered the house speciality: SEVEN FLAVOURS OF YUM.

It was whisker-licking-good!

I had just started on the second layer of my ice cream – mascarpone and mint – when I heard a voice whisper, "Hey you! Pssst!"

HOLEY CHEESE – I thought I recognised that voice! I turned around but didn't see anyone. So I shrugged, picked up my spoon, and dug into the ice cream again.

Hey! Pssst!

"Hey, you! Pssst! Pssst! I'm talking to you!"

I turned again, but the only thing I saw was an **enormouse** plastic banana-flavoured ice cream cone. Strange.

I was about to take another bite of ice cream when someone **smacked** me on the back so hard that I ended up **SNOUT-DEEP** in my bowl. "Geronimo, I've called you three times now!"

CRUSTY CAT LITTER!

After I wiped the mascarpone and mint ice cream out of my eyes, I turned around for the third time.

I saw a familiar snout with **huge teeth** pop out of the plastic banana-flavoured ice cream cone.

"Pssst, it's me – Hercule Poirat! Do you like my disguise?"

"Hercule?" I whispered in surprise. "What are you doing here?"

"I'm **investigating**," he explained. "I want you to keep your eyes wide open. There's a **mystery** apaw, Geronimo, and I need you to help me solve it!"

Hercule Poirat is a famouse private detective and one of my good friends. He's always trying to get me involved in his crazy investigations!

I couldn't help being intrigued. "What kind of mystery is it this time?"

"I don't know yet," Hercule said, lowering his voice to a whisper. "But stay on your paws, keep your eyes wide open, and be alert! Got it, Geronimo?"

I squeaked, "How can I be alert if I don't even know what I'm supposed to be looking for?"

But Hercule had already **VANISHED**!

Bugsy and Benjamin hadn't noticed anything. They were too busy gobbling up their ice cream! When they got to the seventh layer – spicy Gorgonzola and

SQUEAK!

You liked it that much, huh?

I felt like such a CHEESEBRAIN!

You did a snoutdive!

chocolate with pistachios – they both squeaked for the seventh time, "**HOLEY CHEESE**, this is soooo good!"

When they finally looked up from their empty cups, they gaped at me with funny looks on their snouts. Then they both burst out laughing!

"You really liked your ice cream, huh, Uncle G?" Benjamin said with a giggle. **"It's all over you! You look like you did a snoutdive right into the cup!"**

HERCULE POIRAT

FIRST NAME: Hercule

LAST NAME: Poirat

WHO HE IS: Geronimo's friend since preschool. He's been playing pranks on Geronimo since they were tiny mouselings!

PROFESSION: Private investigator. He runs the Poirat Agency.

HOBBIES: He has a real passion for jokes and disguises. He loves to surprise Geronimo while wearing different costumes.

HIS DREAM: To fight evil!

HIS BATTLE CRY: "Have no fear, Hercule Poirat is here!"

HIS SECRET: He loves to eat bananas because he thinks they cure everything, from colds to calluses!

News Flash!

I took Benjamin and Bugsy home, then scampered back to my house. **RANCID RICOTTA**, I was so sticky from the ice cream that an annoying swarm of mosquitoes had begun BUZZING all around me! To get rid of them, I took a warm shower, scrubbed my fur with mozzarella-scented soap, and finished with a dusting of fresh cheese-scented powder.

Once I was clean, I wandered into the kitchen for a snack. I made myself a TRIPLE-DECKER CHEESE SANDWICH, along with a **huge** mozzarella milkshake. Yum!

I turned on the TV to watch the news and began **nibbling** on my sandwich. But what I heard the reporter say almost made me *choke* on my cheese!

"Alarming news flash from New Mouse City, Mouse Island's capital," he began. "It seems that rodents there have been struck by a bizarre disease – a disease that is very contagious and produces strange **BLUE SPOTS**! The best scientists in New Mouse City are currently looking into this bizarre phenomenon. Stay tuned to Rat TV for the latest!"

I turned off the TV, gobbled down my food, and got dressed faster than a rat with a cat on his tail. Then I called The Rodent's Gazette office. Everyone there sounded totally rattled!

Before I could squeak, Priscilla Prettywhiskers shouted, "Boss! Where are you? Did you hear about the **BLUE SPOTS**? What do you want us to do?"

"Priscilla, shake a paw and get all the editors together for an **emergency meeting**!" I said.

I hung up and called Mayor Frederick Fuzzypaws, one of my old friends. He cried, "Geronimo! I need your help to reassure New Mouse City's rodents about this **BLUE SPOT** breakout. I'm counting on you!"

The next rodent I called was Thea, who also shouted in my ear. "**Geronimo!** Did you hear the news about the BLUE SPOTS?"

BOSS!

"Of course I did!" I squeaked. "I need you to call all our friends and family except for Grandfather. Have them meet us at The Rodent's Gazette office in two shakes of a mouse's tail!"

I hung up and hightailed it to The Rodent's Gazette. Out on the street, I was struck squeakless. It looked like many rodents had already reacted to the emergency — and they'd taken matters into their own paws in all sorts of different ways!

Geronimo!

First, a **strange mouse** wearing a wetsuit, goggles, and a snorkel accidentally stepped on my tail.

Did you hear the news?

Another was walking on stilts — to breathe cleaner air, he said — and another had wrapped himself in aluminium foil. One rodent had even smeared herself with a concoction made of rotten Gorgonzola cheese. She was surrounded by a CLOUD OF FLIES! Rats, what a smell!

Pinching my snout, I asked, "Escuze be. Why bid yu zbear yurzelf wid rodded Corconzola?" (Translation: "Excuse me. Why did you smear yourself with rotten Gorgonzola?")

She answered, "Mr. Stilton, I thought it was obvious the smell keeps the GERMS away! Know who told me? My furdresser's mother-in-law's friend's ..."

But I stopped listening when I spotted Trap. He was wearing a deepwater diver's helmet! He started talking to me, but with that helmet over his snout, I couldn't hear a single word. I stared at his mouth, and after a while I figured out what he was saying by reading his lips.

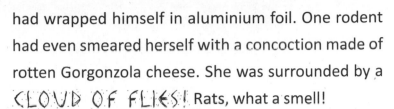

"You'll catch the BLUE SPOTS! Nah-nah-nah-nah-nah!" he sang. **"I have this helmet, so I don't have to worry!"**

39

AN ENORMOUSLY IMPORTANT CAKE

When I arrived at The Rodent's Gazette, the conference room was packed! We had to put a double row of chairs around the table so that everyone could fit.

Everyone was there – the staff of The Rodent's Gazette, plus all of my friends and relatives, including Grandfather William! **CHEESE AND CRACKERS!** I had left instructions not to tell him about the meeting, but there he was in the front row.

Grandfather always manages to find out about everything. And when there's an emergency, he scampers back to The Rodent's Gazette and takes control! As soon as he saw me, he squeaked, "There's no time to waste! The city is in chaos, and the **BLUE SPOTS** are

Grandfather William

popping up everywhere. Get your tail in gear!"

Trap jumped up and showed us a sign that he had written. It said, **HERE'S THE SOLUTION: A GOOD HELMET. TA-DA!**

"Trap, I don't think that's going to work," I said, scratching my snout. "We can't live with helmets over our snouts all the time. We need to find a **real solution**!"

"Well said, Grandson! You do seem somewhat intelligent when you try," Grandfather William said. "And because I'm always a paw ahead of you, I've

Professor Brainymouse

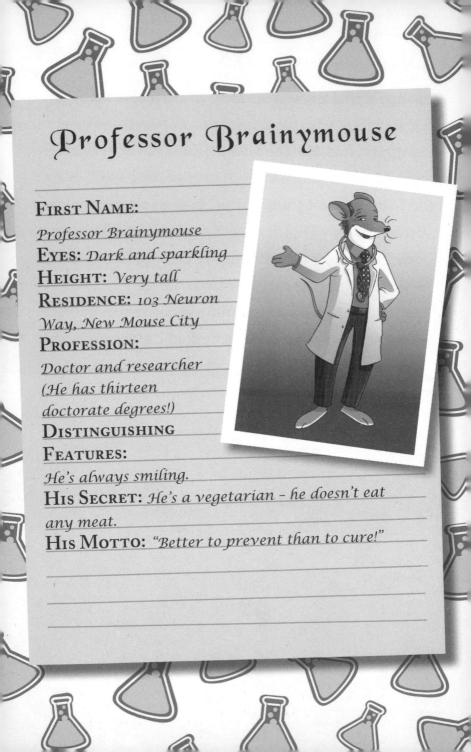

FIRST NAME:
Professor Brainymouse
EYES: *Dark and sparkling*
HEIGHT: *Very tall*
RESIDENCE: *103 Neuron Way, New Mouse City*
PROFESSION:
Doctor and researcher (He has thirteen doctorate degrees!)
DISTINGUISHING FEATURES:
He's always smiling.
HIS SECRET: *He's a vegetarian – he doesn't eat any meat.*
HIS MOTTO: *"Better to prevent than to cure!"*

already asked my friend Professor Brainymouse to find the solution!"

Only then did I notice the intelligent-looking rodent seated next to my grandfather. He cleared his throat and squeaked, "Rodents, diving helmets and other **do-it-yourself remedies** don't work! To fight this strange disease, we first have to pinpoint exactly what it is. Once we know that, then we find the cure!"

Trap shrugged and held up another sign: I'LL NEVER TAKE OFF THE HELMET! YOU NEVER KNOW WHAT COULD HAPPEN. I DON'T WANT TO GET SICK!

Mouldy mozzarella, once my cousin gets a **FUR-BRAINED** idea in his head, there's no stopping him!

"What about us?" asked Thea.

Here's a little list ...

"What can The Rodent's Gazette do?"

Professor Brainymouse smiled. "You can do a lot! Here's a little list ..."

I quickly read his list and announced, "No problem. We'll take care of getting the **most crucial** information out to the citizens of New Mouse City!"

The professor got up and squeaked, "Thank you! In the meantime, I'll **scurry over** to the laboratory and start on the research immediately. Professor von Volt, Doc, and a group of the **BEST RESEARCHERS** in New Mouse

Here's what The Rodent's Gazette will do:

1) Keep rodents informed by printing a special edition of The Rodent's Gazette detailing how everyone should respond to this crisis.
2) Raise funds to finance the research.
3) Write, copy, and distribute flyers detailing key steps that all rodents should follow:
- Always wash paws with soap and water.
- Eat plenty of fruits and vegetables to strengthen the immune system.
- Keep calm and contact your doctor with questions.

City are waiting for me!"

As soon as I heard the name Doc, I blushed and stammered, "Er ... I–I–I would be happy to go with you. So that I can ... keep the readers up to date with the progress of my engage – I mean, the progress of the research!"

Professor Brainymouse looked at me like I had **THREE SNOUTS**! He checked my eyes, checked my

Hmmm ... tongue-tied!

Hee, hee, hee!

pulse, took my blood pressure, and ordered me to open my mouth.

"Hmmm ... white eyeballs, high blood pressure, red ears, pink cheeks, **wobbly legs**, tongue-tied. There's no doubt! It's a bad case of —"

RANCID RICOTTA! I quickly interrupted him.

"Professor, tell me the truth!" I begged, twisting my tail. "Do I have a bad case of BLUE SPOT DISEASE?"

"No, nothing that serious. You're as healthy as fresh sharp Cheddar!" He winked and whispered, **"Mr. Stilton, you've got ... a bad crush!"**

WHAT A FABUMOUSE TEAM!

Grandfather William stared at me over the top of his glasses and exclaimed, "**A CRUSH?** How silly! Geronimo, don't you dare make me look bad in front of my friend. Get your tail in gear! For now, I'll leave you in charge – but if you don't shape up, I'll take over! Understand?"

I promised my grandfather I'd do my very best. **CHATTERING CHEDDAR**, what else could I say? As soon as he and Professor Brainymouse left, I was ready to get to work. There was so much to do, but I couldn't let it **RUFFLE MY FUR**!

My entire staff and all my friends wanted to help. First, I noted every mouse's age and skill. Then Patty Plumprat helped

Get your tail in gear!

WHAT A FABUMOUSE TEAM

Trap kept us all laughing with his jokes!

Ho, ho, ho!

Bruce Hyena suggested some exercises to keep the residents of New Mouse City in shape.

Here we go!

Heh, heh, heh!

Ha, ha, ha!

My staff made flyers that explained how to strengthen the body's immune system and avoid infection.

What do you think?

Is everything ready?

Let's go!

STAMP

Uncle Samuel S. Stingysnout wanted to be in charge of raising money to finance the research. Since he's known for his stinginess, I decided that Aunt Sweetfur (the most generous mouse in my family) should work with him. Wild Willie and OOK, both experts in martial arts, also joined the fundraising team. They were ready, willing, and able to protect the money we raised!

Don't touch!

Tina Spicytail prepared healthy fruit and vegetable drinks for everyone!

Freshly squeezed drinks, anyone?

me organise everything that needed to be done. Soon, every rodent had been given a specific task.

What a **FABUMOUSE** team!

Trap, Thea, Benjamin, and Bugsy Wugsy offered to come with me to Professor Brainymouse's lab and see how the research was going. Thea was in charge of taking photos, Benjamin and Bugsy were writing a blog to keep our readers informed about the progress, and Trap – well, Trap kept us all **laughing** with his jokes.

Together, we headed to the Academy of Science, New Mouse City's top scientific university. Professor Brainymouse's team was holed up there, working

So many scholars . . . and scientists!

Awesome!

around the clock to find a cure for the STRANGE **BLUE** SPO**T**S. The campus had been recently built in a brand-new neighbourhood on the outskirts of New Mouse City. It wasn't even on the map yet, but everyone already called it the `Science Quarter`!

The academy had the most modern science laboratories and the biggest science library on Mouse Island. The **_very best of the best_** researchers worked and studied there. **MOUSERIFIC!**

At the campus entrance, a tall, athletic mouse wearing an oversized lab coat greeted us with a bright smile.

NICE TO MEET YOU, RICK!

"I bet you're Mr. Stilton!" he squeaked. "I'm Richard Curlytail, assistant and researcher. **Call me Rick!** This way, please. The professor is waiting for you!"

Thea shook his paw. "Nice to meet you, Rick — I'm Thea, and this is Benjamin, Bugsy Wugsy, and Trap."

"Welcome! For safety and security reasons, please put on these coats." After giving us lab coats, he handed each of us a small card and squeaked, "Here! These are your ID badges. **Keep them on you at all times!"**

SERIOUS SECURITY!

Rick led us through some big rooms, courtyards, warehouses, and stairwells until we finally came to Professor Brainymouse's laboratory. He made us all walk single file on a yellow line as a high-tech camera scanned our eyes. **RAT-MUNCHING RATTLESNAKES**, this was some serious security!

Suddenly, five mechanical arms popped out of the ceiling, all holding huge pairs of tweezers. They plucked a whisker from each of us. *Yow!* Holey cheese, that hurt!

"Sorry about the whiskers," Rick apologised. "But it's a necessary precaution! Now the security system will recognise your eyes and your DNA."*

I nodded. "I understand. I've been in some **top secret** scenarios before!"

"Listen up, everyone!" Rick squeaked. "Professor Brainymouse's lab requires the highest level of security. Do you understand?"

He lowered his voice. "The professor has even given this project a special code name: the **Cheese Experiment**. That way, other mice won't know what he and his team are working on!"

Once we were all suited up, Rick entered the access code on a keypad, and the door to the laboratory opened. He escorted us into the lab, where Professor Brainymouse waved in welcome.

"Welcome to the **Cheese Experiment**!" he whispered with a wink. "Let me show you around. But please, be very quiet. It's important not to distract the researchers! They're working on very complicated experiments, and they need to keep their snouts down and focus."

*DNA is the genetic code. It is unique for every living thing.

He turned to me. "Mr. Stilton, be sure to take good notes. Your grandfather asked me to keep an eye on you! It's important that your readers are well informed."

"Of course," I quickly answered. "I respect my readers!"

I pulled out a notebook and began to scribble. First, I wrote down the name and **special skills** of each researcher.

I spotted Professor Paws von Volt and his nephew

PROFESSOR PAWS VON VOLT   Dewey von Volt   RICK CURLYTAIL   Wanda McSlice

Professor Paws von Volt and his nephew Dewey are inventors and scientists. They specialise in time travel!

Rick Curlytail is a brilliant biologist. Wanda McSlice is a bit of a mystery mouse, but she's very smart and capable.

Dewey, along with Vivian von Volt, Professor Astrofur, and Dr. Swisswhiskers.

There were other young researchers in the lab, too, including a **striking** rodent with platinum blonde fur and icy blue eyes whom I had never seen before. Her name was Wanda McSlice, and she was a `biotechnologist` with a scholarship paid by a company named Cheese, Inc.

And, naturally, Doc was there, too.

Dr. Swisswhiskers   PROFESSOR ASTROFUR   Dr. Bitmouse, aka Doc   VIVIAN VON VOLT

Dr. Swisswhiskers is a scientist specialising in warts and spots. Astrofur is a great professor!

Vivian von Volt is a philosopher and an expert in bioethics. Doc is unique – brilliant, funny, and as sharp as good Cheddar!

Squeak! My tail trembled and my fur stood on end!
I was so excited that when I walked past her, I tripped on the leg of a stool. I spun on my paws, did a double flip, landed flat on my belly, and smacked my snout on the floor! **Bang!**

LABORATORY · SAFETY

In science laboratories, it is very important to follow strict guidelines. These guidelines are for everyone's safety and protection. Lab coats, gloves, goggles, masks, and special hoods are some of the precautions that may be required to avoid exposure to dangerous substances. Laboratories can be subdivided into safety levels; each level is based on the degree of danger it poses and the kind of work under way.

FORMING A RESEARCH TEAM

A research team can be made up of researchers specialising in various areas. This is helpful because there are often many different kinds of problems to solve! There may be biologists, physicists, chemists, and doctors all on one team. Even philosophers and experts in bioethics can be part of the team!

GOOD NEWS

All the researchers turned to look at me, and I blushed from the ends of my ears to the tip of my tail.

"Shhh! Geronimo, couldn't you stay on your paws for once?" Thea scolded me.

Trap flicked my ear with a grin. "Try not to be such a **CHEESEBRAIN**, Cuz!"

Just then Wanda McSlice jumped to her paws and screeched, "Rotten rats' teeth! I can't work with all this noise!"

ROTTEN RATS' TEETH!

She stormed out, slamming the door behind her. She certainly had her tail in a twist!

"She's a little edgy," Rick explained,

"but she's **the best in her field**."

Doc gave him a wry look as she walked over and pinched me on the cheek.

"Here's my little cheese puff — I heard you coming! It was the familiar smack on the floor that gave you away!"

Cheese niblets, how embarrassing! "I-I-I didn't trip!" I stammered. "I-I wanted to ... um ... see if the floor was clean!"

I was a mess! Luckily, the professor stepped in and asked us to follow him to the conference room for an important announcement.

Professor Brainymouse sat down behind a large desk, cleared his throat, and said, "Dear colleagues, I have good news and bad news. Which do you want to hear first?"

"THE GOOD NEWS!" we all exclaimed.

The professor nodded grimly. "The good news is

Here's my little cheese puff!

that I discovered the name of this mysterious **BLUE SPOT DISEASE** while I was looking through a very old book. The disease is called **RODENTIA SPOTILITIS!**" He looked at me. "Did you get that, Geronimo?"

"Yes!" I said, my pen flying across the page. "So what's the bad news?"

"The bad news is that there's no cure – so it's up to us to find one. Rick will give you all the research protocol!* Good luck!"

The scientists scampered out of the room.

I sat there reviewing my notes and minding my own business when – **JUMPING JACK CHEESE!** A cactus plant pricked me!

YOW!

Pssst ...

"Yow!" I squeaked, leaping to my paws.

"Pssst, Geronimo!" the plant whispered. "It's me, Hercule! Did you like my little prank?"

*Research protocol is a detailed description of phases and procedures that every researcher must follow carefully.

RODENTIA SPOTILITIS

WHAT IT IS: A very rare disease, described hundreds of years ago in an ancient document titled 'The Mysterious Blue Spot Disease'. Now the condition is better known as rodentia spolilitis.

SYMPTOMS: Blue spots all over the body – especially on the snout!

HOW IT EVOLVES: If not addressed, it causes rigidity of the tail. If left untreated for too long, it can even cause the tail to fall off!

CAUSE: Unknown!

CURE: Unknown!

CURRENT PLAN: Analyse the blue spots; find the cause of the disease; find the cure.

Research Protocol for Studying
BLUE SPOT DISEASE aka
RODENTIA SPOTILITIS

Blue spot removed.

This is what it looks like under the microscope

HEY, THERE!

1. Remove the blue spot from a rodent's snout.

2. Examine the spot under a microscope. Observe how it grows and how cells are reproduced.

3. Try to make the spot respond by using the most powerful cures known to mice:

Gorgonzolite concentrate

Parmesano acid

Various kinds of raticillin

UGH, THAT STINKS!

YUM!

YIKES!

I sighed. "No, I didn't! MY TAIL IS FULL OF THORNS!"

"Well, it's time to get your tail in gear. From this moment on, I want you to keep an eye on the researchers — don't let them out of your sight for a second! Because they are working day and night, you have to stay awake day and night."

THUNDERING CAT TAILS! "What if I have to go to the bathroom, or if I feel sleepy, or if I get hungry?" I protested.

"Geronimo, this is important!" Hercule squeaked. "If you're hungry, have some **banana sweets**. They'll give you energy!" He shoved a pawful of the sweets into my mouth.

Yuck!

EYES OPEN DAY AND NIGHT

From then on, I kept my eyes wide open day and night, just like Hercule instructed.

Professor Brainymouse and his scientists worked around the clock. They worked every second of the day and – **squeak!** – every second of the night, too. They would have forgotten to eat if Tina hadn't come

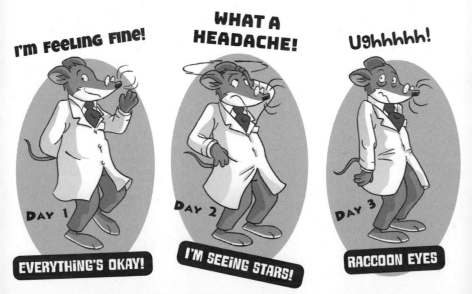

by every day with a pan full of **triple-cheese lasagne** to keep us all going!

The first day went pretty well. The second day, I started seeing stars. The third day, I had raccoon eyes. The fourth day, I looked like a zombie. By the fifth day, I was an **enormouse mess**!

But the researchers were so engrossed in the Cheese Experiment, they never seemed to get tired! That was one tough team of mice!

That night, Wanda McSlice and Doc worked side by side in the lab. They didn't look the least bit tired – not a single *drooping whisker* between them!

ARGH!

DAY 4

I LOOKED LIKE A ZOMBIE!

Triple-cheese lasagne?

Squeak!

DAY 5

I WAS AN ENORMOUSE MESS!

I tried to keep my eyes open, but I was getting soooooo sleepy. I tried drinking fifteen cups of tea to keep myself awake, but they didn't help at all! **CHEESE NIBLETS!**

In the dead of night, Professor Brainymouse came to check on how the work was going. He even brought me the ancient book that talked about **BLUE SPOT DISEASE**.

"I think you'll like it, Geronimo. It's fascinating! I know you have a passion for old books."

Just then Doc squeaked, "Professor Brainymouse, I just made a **MOUSERIFIC** discovery!"

The professor and Doc scurried into a corner to talk. Every so often, I could hear the professor cry out:

"Fabumouse!" **"AMAZING!"** *"Mousetastic!"*

For a second, it seemed like Wanda McSlice was trying to eavesdrop on their conversation, but it was probably just my imagination. After all, she was on their team. Why would she need to eavesdrop?

With a shrug, I began flipping through the old book.

CHEESE AND CRACKERS – for a while, I forgot how tired I was! The book really was fabumouse. It described the symptoms of BLUE SPOT DISEASE and explained how it had spread many, many, many years ago. But it didn't say anything about a cause or a possible cure.

As I read, I noticed that some pages were missing. It looked like pages had been torn from the book. **How strange!** But then again, the book was incredibly old. The pages may have just fallen out over time … right?

As I thought about it, I felt my eyelids growing heavier … and heavier … and heavier.
Then, without realising it, I fell fast asleep!

A TOTAL, ABSOLUTE, DOWNRIGHT DISASTER!

When I finally woke up, I was tied to the swivel chair like a mummy. **SLIMY SWISS CHEESE!** A voice was squeaking urgently in my ear. "Wake up!"

I slowly opened my eyes. Standing in front of me was ... Hercule! Phew!

He untied me. Then, with his paws on his hips and a stern expression on his snout, he said, "Geronimo! What happened? Didn't I tell you to keep your eyes open? I have to go, but meet me at the Cheese, Inc. factory in an hour. There's definitely something funny going on!"

I finally looked around and noticed that the entire laboratory was in **shambles**: upside-down test tubes, broken equipment, flooded floors ...

It was a total, absolute, downright disaster!

And in one corner, also tied up like a mummy, was Doc. She had a **huge lump** on her head and was completely unconscious. **Whiskers wobbling**, I scurried over to free her.

When I reached her, she opened her eyes and said, "My hero! Maybe you're not a **CHEESEBRAIN** after all!"

My snout turned red. "Hero?" I tried to focus. "What happened? Who clunked you on the head? Did you see anyone?"

"Unfortunately, I didn't see a thing!" she squeaked. "I had just finished telling the professor that I had found a possible cure for **RODENTIA SPOTILITIS**. When he left, I turned back to my work. A second later, I felt a thump and blacked out ..."

Wait one whisker-licking minute – Wanda McSlice had disappeared! **How strange!** Without wasting another moment, I set off the alarm.

Woowooowoooooooooooooooooooooooooooo!

The alarm was the only way to alert all the scientists that something had happened!

Professor Brainymouse was the first to arrive. "What's going on?" he squeaked urgently. "A fire? A flood? A gas leak?"

"A total, absolute, downright disaster!" I cried.

Soon, all the rodents on campus gathered in the emergency meeting place – the courtyard. The only one missing was Wanda McSlice. **How strange!**

77

Benjamin, Bugsy Wugsy, and Thea were there. I gave them each a reassuring hug. "Don't get your tails in a twist! Everything's under control ... almost."

Thea and I helped the professor inspect the laboratories. Unfortunately, everything was **DESTROYED**: the microscopes, the computers, the notes!

It was a total, absolute, downright disaster!

Rats – it was going to be impossible to move ahead with the **Cheese Experiment**!

Only someone **TRULY EVIL** could have

What happened?

WE'RE COMING!

destroyed all the work that so many rodents' tails depended on. (We rodents are **very protective** of our tails!)

At that moment, I felt a tug on my jacket. It was Benjamin and Bugsy.

"Uncle G, we have an idea," Benjamin said.

"Professor Brainymouse and his team could use the labs at our school!" Bugsy exclaimed. "Think about it: they're brand new, and they have cutting-edge computers and microscopes, too!"

AN ABSOLUTE DISASTER!

Here we are! What happened?

HOLEY CHEESE! It was a truly fabumouse idea! I hugged them both. "**MOUSETASTIC THINKING** – I'm proud of you! Maybe there's still hope for a cure ..."

WANT A BANANA?

Quick as a mouse on a cheese hunt, I called the school principal and New Mouse City's mayor to get permission to use the school laboratories.

Professor Brainymouse and his colleagues headed for the school to resume their research. In the meantime, I scurried to meet Hercule at the Cheese, Inc. factory. I ducked behind a banana plant and peeked at the factory – but as I did, **THE PLANT SPOKE!**

"Psssssst! Hey, Geronimo, want a banana?"

ACK! It was Hercule again!

He signalled for me to be quiet. Then he reached into the pocket of his yellow trench coat and pulled out a pair of powerful binoculars and a strange listening device he had invented to hear distant conversations. He gave them to me and whispered, "Here, Geronimo. **Something suspicious** is happening down there, or

81

my name isn't Hercule Poirat!"

I put on the headphones and pointed the binoculars towards an open window on the first floor. **DOUBLE-TWISTED RATTAILS!** I couldn't believe my eyes ...

In a room on the first floor of the Cheese, Inc. factory, I spotted none other than Sally Ratmousen and ... Wanda McSlice!

I see them!

SALLY RATMOUSEN

83

Wanda McSlice

In Wanda's paws, I could see the scientists' notes and a test tube full of liquid. **RANCID RICOTTA!** I turned on my headphones and listened carefully.

"Good job!" Sally said. "You were right to destroy the **Cheese Experiment**. Doc was about to discover the cure for rodentia spotilitis — but we need to keep it to ourselves! With it, we can ransom all the infected mice. They'll have to give us an **enormouse** pile of gold or ... goodbye, tails!"

Wanda McSlice squeaked, "Yes, but don't forget it was my idea to spread RODENTIA SPOTILITIS throughout the city. I was the one who found the description of

the disease in that ancient library book. I was the one to infiltrate the labs. I was the one to stop Professor Brainymouse's team!"

Sally squeaked, "**HOW DARE YOU!** This is my factory! I built it, I prepared the concentrate to spread the rodentia spotilitis, and I had my planes spray it across the city! It was all me!"

ROTTEN RATS' TEETH! What horrible rodents! We had to stop them – and fast!

Without thinking twice, Hercule and I ran to the building, leaped through the window, and bounded into the room.

Hercule bellowed fiercely, **"HERCUUUULE POIRAAAAT IS HEEEERE!"**

Then he added, "We got you!"

But Sally and Wanda burst out laughing.

"Ha, ha, ha! Try to stop us, cheesebrains!" Sally sneered. "Rodentia spotilitis is everywhere, and we're the only ones with the cure. **Either we get a sack of gold, or you can say goodbye to your tails!"**

LET'S TEACH THOSE RATS A LESSON!

Whiskers trembling with anger, I squeaked, "Shame on you, Sally! And Dr. McSlice, you should be **ashamed**, too – a scientist should never behave like this!"

"Actually, I'm not a scientist," she squeaked with a sly smile. "I'm not even Wanda McSlice!"

She pulled off her wig and top layer of clothing. **HOLEY CHEESE** – it was the Shadow!

First Name: The Shadow
Last Name: Ratmousen
Who She Is: Sally Ratmousen's cousin
Profession: The most notorious thief in New Mouse City! She's willing to do anything to get rich.
Unusual Characteristics: She's known for her clever disguises. She uses a different disguise for every job!

"And I'm not Sally!" the other rodent added, tearing off her disguise, too — it was the nefarious Sleezer!

First Name: Sleezer
Last Name: No one knows
Who He Is: A true mystery —
no one is sure who he is!
Profession: The most evil,
troublemaking rodent on
all of Mouse Island
Unusual Characteristics:
He usually wears a dark trench coat and a
large-brimmed hat to hide his snout.

Before Hercule and I could even squeak, the two thieves jumped out the window, shouting, "Remember! We want a stack of cash or **goodbye, tails**! We'll be contacting the mayor soon!"

We chased them as fast as our paws would carry us. We were closing in when a helicopter appeared out of nowhere and lowered a rope. Sleezer and the Shadow quickly grabbed on.

As they flew away, they cried, "Try catching us now, **CHEDDARHEADS**!"

Suddenly, we heard a noise in the room we had just left. It seemed to be coming from inside a cabinet. We flung the cabinet door open – and found Sally Ratmousen inside!

"IT'S ABOUT TIME!" she squeaked with a sigh. "Thank you, Geronimo! Wanda

McSlice – I mean, the Shadow – locked me in here after she tricked me into funding her research!"

"I'm so happy you're not working with that AWFUL SEWER RAT, Sally –" I began.

But Sally interrupted me. "I am, and will always be, your **ENEMY**! This is just a short truce, for the good of all mice. Then we'll go back to being enemies, just like before!"

I shook her paw. "You're one of my competitors, but you will never be an **ENEMY**! But fine. Truce!"

Hercule reached into his trench coat and pulled out

It's Sally!

a tray holding three glasses of banana smoothie.

"How about we toast to it?" he squeaked.

As we toasted, I noticed that the Shadow had dropped two sheets of paper ...

This is just a short truce!

CHEESE AND CRACKERS – these were the pages torn out of the old rodentia spotilitis book! And they

RODENTIA SPOTILITIS

seems to be related to the blue garlic of Ratzikistan!

I have often observed that patients who contract rodentia spotilitis had come into contact with this species of malodorous garlic. Typically, the patients were farmers, those unloading merchandise, and peasants who had inadvertently ingested a piece.

contained **enormousely** important information!
This could almost certainly help Professor Brainymouse
find a cure.

We jumped into Hercule's Bananamobile and
zoomed to the school laboratories.

"Faster, Hercule, faster!" Sally urged. **"Let's teach
those sewer rats a lesson they won't forget!"**

Faster!
Faster!

FRIENDS TOGETHER!
MICE FOREVER!

A few moments later, we pulled up in front of Benjamin and Bugsy Wugsy's school. We **HIGHTAILED** it to the laboratory, frantically waving the two missing pages from the old book on **BLUE SPOT DISEASE**.

Professor Brainymouse scampered towards us, took the pages in his paws, and stared at them for a long time, murmuring, "Hmm ... interesting ..."

Without squeaking another word, he closed himself inside the lab with his team.

When he finally came out, he announced, "Friends, we found the cure for **BLUE SPOT DISEASE** – but it needs to be administered

WE HAVE A CURE!

within a few hours or it will be too late!"

"Give it to me!" cried Sally. "I can produce an **enormouse** amount of it in my factory!"

"And I'll use my plane to spray it over the city," Thea added.

"And I'll keep morale high with my **FABUMOUSE** jokes!" Trap exclaimed. (I tried not to roll my eyes.)

"I'll get out a newsflash about the cure!" I squeaked.

Doc piped up, too. "And I'll take care of organising a giant party to get as many mice as possible in one place!"

We all put our paws together and shouted, "Friends together! Mice forever!"

We scampered off as fast as our paws would take us. With Benjamin and Bugsy's help, I wrote a long article for The Rodent's Gazette titled The Cheese Experiment. Our readers needed to know the whole truth about BLUE SPOT DISEASE, not to mention Sleezer and the Shadow's blackmail plans!

Once my article was finished and sent to the printer, I remembered that I had barely closed my eyes in days.

I was sleepier than a marathon mouse!

I suddenly felt my eyelids become heavier, and heavier, and heavier! I spotted Thea flying over the city in her plane before I fell asleep with a thump.

ZZZZZZZZZ!

When I woke up, Hercule's snout was right in my face. Standing next to him were Thea, Trap, Benjamin, Bugsy Wugsy, and Professor Brainymouse — all staring at me with worried looks on their snouts. **How strange!**

I touched my face and — cheese niblets! — felt a huge bump on the tip of my snout. "Nooooo! A **BLUE** SPOT!"

I almost fainted from fright, but Trap burst out laughing.

"You're such a **CHEESEBRAIN**, Cousin!" he said. "Did you like my little joke? It's just a fake spot — the **RODENTIA SPOTILITIS** has been cured!"

98

It was a horrible joke, but I was so relieved that I couldn't stay angry. I burst out laughing.

"Thundering cattails — let's party!"

And so the **Cheese Experiment** came to an end with a bit of a scare, a laugh, and a party with good friends.

It was a **FABUMOUSE** adventure — but we never would have discovered the cure if we hadn't worked together. After all, every problem has a solution — and together, we can find it!

So long until my **NEXT ADVENTURE**!

Your friend,

Geronimo Stilton

THE RODENT'S GAZETTE

1. Main entrance
2. Printing presses (where everything is printed)
3. Accounts department
4. Editorial room (where editors, illustrators, and designers work)
5. Geronimo Stilton's office
6. Geronimo's botanical garden

MAP OF NEW MOUSE CITY

1. Industrial Zone
2. Cheese Factories
3. Angorat International Airport
4. WRAT Radio and Television Station
5. Cheese Market
6. Fish Market
7. Town Hall
8. Snotnose Castle
9. The Seven Hills of Mouse Island
10. Mouse Central Station
11. Trade Centre
12. Movie Theatre
13. Gym
14. Catnegie Hall
15. Singing Stone Plaza
16. The Gouda Theatre
17. Grand Hotel
18. Mouse General Hospital
19. Botanical Gardens
20. Cheap Junk for Less (Trap's store)
21. Parking Lot
22. Mouseum of Modern Art
23. University and Library
24. The Daily Rat
25. The Rodent's Gazette
26. Trap's House
27. Fashion District
28. The Mouse House Restaurant
29. Environmental Protection Centre
30. Harbour Office
31. Mousidon Square Garden
32. Golf Course
33. Swimming Pool
34. Blushing Meadow Tennis Courts
35. Curlyfur Island Amusement Park
36. Geronimo's House
37. Historic District
38. Public Library
39. Shipyard
40. Thea's House
41. New Mouse Harbour
42. Luna Lighthouse
43. The Statue of Liberty
44. Hercule Poirat's Office
45. Petunia Pretty Paws's House
46. Grandfather William's House

MAP OF MOUSE ISLAND

1. Big Ice Lake
2. Frozen Fur Peak
3. Slipperyslopes Glacier
4. Coldcreeps Peak
5. Ratzikistan
6. Transratania
7. Mount Vamp
8. Roastedrat Volcano
9. Brimstone Lake
10. Poopedcat Pass
11. Stinko Peak
12. Dark Forest
13. Vain Vampires Valley
14. Goosebumps Gorge
15. The Shadow Line Pass
16. Penny-Pincher Castle
17. Nature Reserve Park
18. Las Ratayas Marinas
19. Fossil Forest
20. Lake Lake
21. Lake Lakelake
22. Lake Lakelakelake
23. Cheddar Crag
24. Cannycat Castle
25. Valley of the Giant Sequoia
26. Cheddar Springs
27. Sulphurous Swamp
28. Old Reliable Geyser
29. Vole Vale
30. Ravingrat Ravine
31. Gnat Marshes
32. Munster Highlands
33. Mousehara Desert
34. Oasis of the Sweaty Camel
35. Cabbagehead Hill
36. Rattytrap Jungle
37. Rio Mosquito
38. Mousefort Beach
39. San Mouscisco
40. Swissville
41. Cheddarton
42. Mouseport
43. New Mouse City
44. Pirate Ship of Cats

THE COLLECTION

HAVE YOU READ ALL OF GERONIMO'S ADVENTURES?

ABOUT THE AUTHOR

Born in New Mouse City, Mouse Island, GERONIMO STILTON is Rattus Emeritus of Mousomorphic Literature and of Neo-Ratonic Comparative Philosophy. For the past twenty years, he has been running The Rodent's Gazette, New Mouse City's most widely read daily newspaper.

Stilton was awarded the Ratitzer Prize for his scoops on *The Curse of the Cheese Pyramid* and *The Search for Sunken Treasure*. He has also received the Andersen Prize

for Personality of the Year. His works have been published all over the globe.

In his spare time, Mr. Stilton collects antique cheese rinds and plays golf. But what he most enjoys is telling stories to his nephew Benjamin.